Robert *Fulton*

Our People

SPIRIT of America®

Robert *Fulton*

Engineer and Inventor

By Pam Rosenberg

The Child's World®
Chanhassen, Minnesota

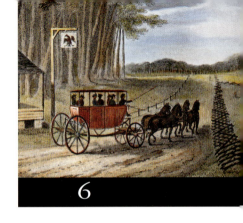

6

Robert *Fulton*

Published in the United States of America by The Child's World®
PO Box 326 • Chanhassen, MN 55317-0326 • 800-599-READ • www.childsworld.com

Acknowledgments
  The Child's World®: Mary Berendes, Publishing Director

  Editorial Directions, Inc.: E. Russell Primm, Emily J. Dolbear, and Pam Rosenberg, Editors; Dawn Friedman, Photo Researcher; Linda S. Koutris, Photo Selector; Sarah E. De Capua, Copy Editor; Susan Ashley, Proofreader; Tim Griffin, Indexer

Photo
  Cover: Bettmann/Corbis; AP/Wide World Photos: 7; Tate Gallery, London/Art Resource, NY: 9; National Portrait Gallery, Smithsonian Institution/Art Resource, NY: 12; The Stapleton Collection/Bridgeman Art Library: 10; Bettmann/Corbis: 2, 15 top, 25; Corbis: 19; Lee Snider/Corbis: 24; Gail Mooney/Corbis: 27; Burstein Collection/Corbis: 28; The Granger Collection, New York: 6, 11, 13, 16, 20, 23, 26; Hulton Archive/Getty Images: 15 bottom, 17, 21; Stock Montage/Getty Images: 18.

Registration
  The Child's World®, Spirit of America®, and their associated logos are the sole property and registered trademarks of The Child's World®.

  Copyright ©2003 by The Child's World®. All rights reserved. No part of this book may be reproduced or utilized in any form or by any means without written permission from the publisher.

Library of Congress Cataloging-in-Publication Data
  Rosenberg, Pam.
    Robert Fulton : engineer and inventor / by Pam Rosenberg.
        p. cm.
    Summary: Discusses the life and work of the inventor who developed the steamboat and made it a commercial success.
    Includes bibliographical references and index.
    ISBN 1-56766-448-2 (Library Bound : alk. paper)
  1. Fulton, Robert, 1765–1815—Juvenile literature. 2. Marine engineers—United States—Biography—Juvenile literature.
  3. Inventors—United States—Biography—Juvenile literature.
  4. Steamboats—United States—History—19th century—Juvenile literature.
  [1. Fulton, Robert, 1765–1815. 2. Inventors. 3. Steamboats—History.]
  I. Title.
    VM140.F9 R67 2003
    623.8'24'092—dc21

2002151722

13   15   26

Contents

Chapter ONE	The Early Years	6
Chapter TWO	From Painting to Submarines	10
Chapter THREE	Creating a Steamboat	18
Chapter FOUR	The North River Steamboat of Clermont	22
	Time Line	29
	Glossary Terms	30
	For Further Information	31
	Index	32

Chapter ONE

The Early Years

IMAGINE LIFE WITHOUT ANY WAY OF GETTING around except walking, riding a horse, or traveling in a horse-drawn wagon. You wouldn't travel far from home too often. When you did decide to take a long trip, it required a lot of planning. Rowboats and sailboats would be the only way to travel on water. It might take weeks, or even months, to get where you wanted to go!

A wagon pulled by horses was one of the few ways to travel in the 1700s.

It seems strange to us now, but in the late 1700s that is exactly how people lived. This way of life wouldn't change until someone invented a way to make travel quicker and easier. There were a few people working on an invention that would change the way people traveled on rivers. Robert Fulton was one of them.

Robert Fulton's parents—Robert Fulton Sr. and Mary Smith Fulton—lived in Lancaster, Pennsylvania. Mr. Fulton worked as a tailor. They had three daughters, Elizabeth, Isabella, and Mary. In early 1765, Mr. Fulton decided to try farming. He purchased a farm in Little Britain Township, about 20 miles (32 kilometers) south of Lancaster. The young Fulton family moved to the farm and began their new life. On November 14, 1765, Mrs. Fulton gave birth to the family's first son. They named him Robert. The Fultons had one more child after Robert. He was named Abraham.

Robert Fulton was born in this farmhouse in 1765.

Unfortunately, the Fultons were not successful at farming. In 1772, their farm was sold at an **auction**. The family moved back to Lancaster, and Robert's father began working as a tailor again. Two years later, Mr. Fulton died, leaving his wife alone to raise five children.

There is not much known about the early years of Robert's life. After his father's death, the family stayed in Lancaster. Robert studied for a time at a school. Then, as a teenager, he moved to the town of Philadelphia. By the time

Interesting Fact

▶ The house where Robert Fulton was born is a national historic site. Visitors can tour the site almost every day throughout the year.

Interesting Fact

▸ Lancaster, Pennsylvania, had a population of about 4,000 at the time Robert Fulton lived there. It was home to many mechanics and fine craftsmen. One famous product that was made in Lancaster was the Conestoga wagon. These wagons were used to carry heavy loads over bad roads. They were pulled by teams of horses.

he was 17, he was working as an **apprentice** to a jeweler named Jeremiah Andrews. It was here that he began painting tiny portraits, called miniatures, on lockets and brooches. He also learned the art of hair working—decorating jewelry with human hair that had been shaped into detailed patterns and pictures.

When Fulton's brother, Abraham, left Lancaster to live in Washington County, Pennsylvania, his mother followed him there. By May 1786, Fulton had saved enough money to buy his mother a farm near Abraham. Soon, around the middle of 1786, Fulton became ill with a terrible cough. His recovery was difficult and he spent some time at a health spa in what is now West Virginia. When he returned to Philadelphia, he continued working as a portrait painter and hair worker.

Fulton began to think about doing something else with his life, however. While he was at the spa, some people had encouraged him to go to England and study art. So, in early 1787, he bought a ticket to sail to England. He left Philadelphia with about $200 and a letter that would introduce him to Benjamin West, a famous American artist who lived in London.

Benjamin West

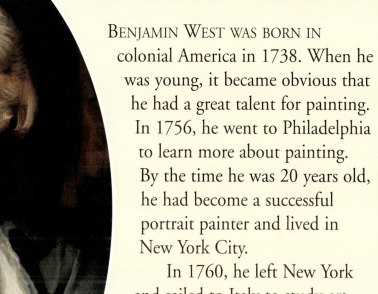

BENJAMIN WEST WAS BORN IN colonial America in 1738. When he was young, it became obvious that he had a great talent for painting. In 1756, he went to Philadelphia to learn more about painting. By the time he was 20 years old, he had become a successful portrait painter and lived in New York City.

In 1760, he left New York and sailed to Italy to study art there. After traveling to many cities in Italy, he settled in London, England, in 1763. He was very talented and liked to paint scenes from history. After a time, he became the official painter of historical subjects for King George III. In 1768, he was one of the founders of Britain's Royal Academy of Arts. West remained in England during the American Revolutionary War (1775–1783), even though he was an American. By that time, he was so successful in England that he did not want to move back to America. He did all he could, though, to help young American men who wanted to be artists. Many of them traveled to London to be taught by West, who called them his "adopted sons." Robert Fulton was one of the artists who benefited from Benjamin West's desire to help young American painters.

Chapter Two

From Painting to Submarines

Fulton went to London in 1787 to study painting.

ROBERT FULTON ARRIVED IN LONDON IN THE spring of 1787. Benjamin West helped him to find a place to stay and gave him advice about painting. Over the next few years, Fulton supported himself by painting portraits. After a while, Fulton decided that even though he had some artistic talent, he would never make his fortune by painting.

At that time, there were many canals being built in England. These manmade waterways were used to carry goods, especially coal and grain, from place to place. It was much easier and less costly to move heavy, bulky items on waterways than over land. Fulton heard stories of people making a lot of money by building canals. He decided to go into canal building, even though he had no training or experience.

In November 1793, Fulton wrote a letter to the earl of Stanhope. The earl was a well-known inventor. He had a plan to build a canal to link the English and Bristol Channels. This plan required the use of **locks**. Fulton wrote to the earl and said that the plan should be to use a series of **inclined planes**. The earl wrote back to Fulton, saying he did not need the advice of someone who had no experience in the field of engineering. So Fulton spent the next three years studying the canals of England. He even applied for a **patent** for his version of the inclined plane. He was given the patent on June 3, 1794.

In late 1794, Fulton moved to Manchester, north of London. Many successful canals had been built in that area. He made some money when he sold a canal plan to the Peak Forest

Many canals that required the use of locks, such as these, were built in England in the late 1700s.

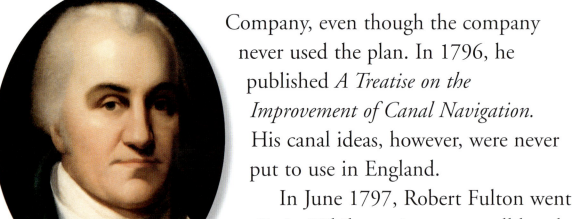

Joel Barlow and his wife Ruth were Fulton's good friends.

Company, even though the company never used the plan. In 1796, he published *A Treatise on the Improvement of Canal Navigation.* His canal ideas, however, were never put to use in England.

In June 1797, Robert Fulton went to Paris. While staying at a small hotel, he met an American woman named Ruth Barlow. Her husband, Joel, was in Algeria, serving as a U.S. **ambassador** to Algeria. They became good friends, and when Joel Barlow returned to Paris, Fulton shared an apartment with the Barlows. It was during this time that Fulton first came up with his ideas for a submarine.

After giving some thought to how he could build a submarine, Fulton approached the French government, hoping it would give him money to build one. The French and British were enemies at the time, so Fulton tried to convince the French government that his submarine could be used to destroy British ships. But the government was not interested. This did not stop Fulton. He tried to convince Napoleón Bonaparte, then commander of the

French army, to use his ideas. When this did not work, he sent the French government his idea again—only this time, he included a submarine model and more details about how it was operated. Still the government was not interested in his plan.

Fulton needed money, so he came up with a new idea. He had seen a panorama in England. This panorama was a large building shaped like a circle. A lifelike scene was painted on the inside walls of the building. People would pay to go inside and see the "panoramic" view. Fulton came up with his own version. In April 1799, he built a tower and painted a lifelike scene inside. The panorama became a popular attraction, and Fulton was finally making money.

Even while working on other projects, however, Fulton never stopped thinking about his submarine. In 1799, after the French government rejected his submarine idea, he presented it to the Dutch government. Its leaders were not interested either, but a

Interesting Fact

▶ Robert Fulton sold the rights to his panorama to an American named James Thayer. The panorama remained open until 1815. Fulton continued to receive a share of the money it made as part of his agreement with Thayer.

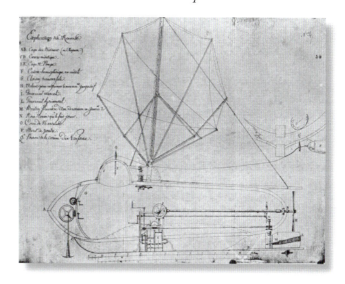

One of Fulton's original drawings of the submarine he hoped to build

13

> ### Interesting Fact

▸ In 1994, five letters that were either written by Robert Fulton or sent to him were auctioned in New York City. They sold for a total of $184,350. Two of the letters sold for $66,300 each. One of them was a letter from James Watt, of Boulton, Watt & Company, to Robert Fulton. It was handwritten by Watt and signed. The letter was about the steam engine the company was building for the *North River Steam Boat*. Part of the letter was a sketch of the engine. The other letter was written by Fulton in 1807 and sent to Robert Livingston. It told Livingston about the *North River Steam Boat's* first trip to Albany, New York.

Dutch citizen named Vanstaphast was. He gave Fulton the money to build one.

Within months, Fulton was ready to test his submarine, the *Nautilus*. On the day of the launch, June 13, 1800, a crowd of people gathered on the banks of the Seine River. Fulton had arranged for Pierre Forfait—the head of the French navy—to be there. Fulton hoped that if his submarine worked, Forfait would convince the French government to support his submarine project.

Fulton took the *Nautilus* out onto the Seine River. He demonstrated how it could travel underwater. Forfait was impressed and gave a good report to General Napoleón Bonaparte.

In November, Fulton was asked to meet with Napoleón. This was the chance he had been waiting for! The meeting went well, and early in 1801, the French government agreed to pay Fulton the money he needed to get the *Nautilus* ready for battle.

By summer 1801, Fulton was ready to try to destroy British ships with his submarine. He was not successful. In addition, the submarine had leaked and was destroyed. That September, he sent a letter to the group over-

Fulton painted this picture of his Nautilus.

seeing his work. He told them although the *Nautilus* was not the success he thought it would be, he had a better idea. If the French government would give him the money to build bigger submarines with a large supply of mines on each, he could destroy all of Britain's ships. Napoleón wanted to see the *Nautilus* himself. This was bad news for Fulton. He had nothing to show for all the money he had received from the French government. Napoleón was angry and believed the French government had been cheated. Fulton was told that French leaders did not want anything more to do with the submarine.

Fulton hoped to convince Napoleón Bonaparte that the French navy should invest in his submarine.

Submarines

ROBERT FULTON WAS NOT THE FIRST PERSON TO THINK ABOUT CREATING an undersea vessel to attack enemy ships. As far back as 1578, a British mathematician named William Bourne wrote about an underwater boat that could be propelled, or moved forward, by oars. His boat was never built. The first submarine to be built was invented by Cornelius van Drebel, a Dutchman. Between 1620 and 1624, he showed people how his submarine worked on England's Thames River. Van Drebel's boat had a wooden frame. The frame was covered with leather. Oars stuck out of its sides, and the openings had flaps made of leather to keep out the water. The oars were used to propel the boat both above and below the water.

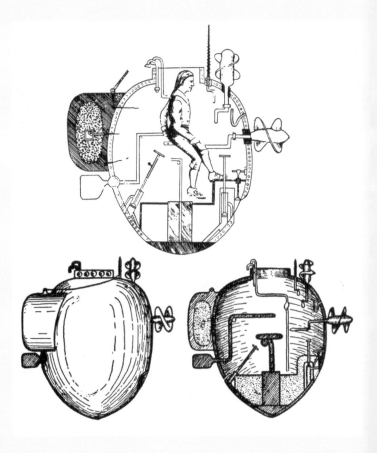

A submarine invented and built in 1775 by a Yale University student named David Bushnell was used unsuccessfully during the American Revolution (1775–1783). His boat, named the *Turtle*, was made of wood. Bushnell powered it by turning a hand crank that was attached to propellers. The submarine was supposed to attach a device containing gunpowder to a

16

British warship's hull. However, the machine that was designed to screw the explosives into the hull of the boat didn't work. The ship's hull was too thick.

Many inventors after Fulton continued to work on making better submarines. By World War I (1914–1918), all countries with large navies had submarines. They played a role during World War I and a larger role in World War II (1939–1945). The first nuclear submarine, the USS *Nautilus*, was put into service in 1954. By the 1960s, all submarines produced for the U.S. Navy were nuclear powered. The nuclear submarine can stay underwater for long periods of time. It can also maintain high speeds for a long time without using up its energy supply.

Chapter **THREE**

Creating a Steamboat

Robert Livingston was a diplomat who played an important role in American history.

IN THE WINTER OF 1802, FULTON SPENT TIME going to dinners and parties with the Barlows and other friends who lived in Paris at the time. At one party, Fulton met a wealthy American **diplomat** named Robert Livingston. The two men had something in common—an interest in building and operating a successful steamboat. They agreed to be partners. In fact, Livingston had been involved in an attempt to build a steamboat several years before. Livingston agreed to pay for the steamboat project. Fulton would build the steamboat.

On October 10, 1802, the two men created a company with the goal of getting a patent for "a new mechanical combination of a boat." The steamboat itself was not a new idea. In 1787, John Fitch had successfully shown how his steamboat worked. Fulton and Livingston, however, hoped to be the first to build a reliable one that would make money. They planned to build a large passenger steamboat that would travel on the Hudson River. It would carry passengers from New York City to Albany, the state capital. Fulton went to work designing a steamboat.

The boat made its first successful run on August 9, 1803. Fulton was finally on the verge of becoming a successful businessman. Sometime in the middle of 1803, though, he met a British secret agent. The agent told him that the British government wanted Fulton to come to London and build his submarine, as well as underwater missiles called torpedoes. Britain was expecting a war with France and wanted to

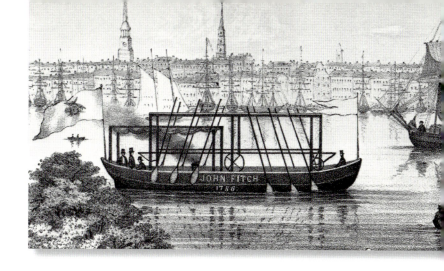

John Fitch demonstrated his steamboat on the Delaware River in 1787.

Interesting Fact

▶ Robert R. Livingston gave the oath of office to George Washington, the first president of the United States. This event took place on April 30, 1789, in New York City.

19

Interesting Fact

▸ The *Nautilus* used its sails for power when it was on the surface. When it was underwater, it was powered by hand-cranked propellers.

keep Fulton from building these underwater weapons for the French. Fulton abandoned his steamboat plans and went to England on July 20, 1804, to build underwater weapons.

While in England, Fulton convinced the British government to allow him to have the engine for his American steamboat built there. This was important to him because Boulton, Watt & Company—a British business—built the best steam engines. By March 1805, the steam engine was ready and Fulton had it shipped to America. Fulton, however, was busy with his underwater mine project. After several unsuccessful attempts to destroy French ships, the British government ended its agreement with Fulton in the summer of 1806. He was disappointed that he had to give up his underwater weapons project, but his work for the British made him rich. Fulton returned to America to continue work on the steamboat project.

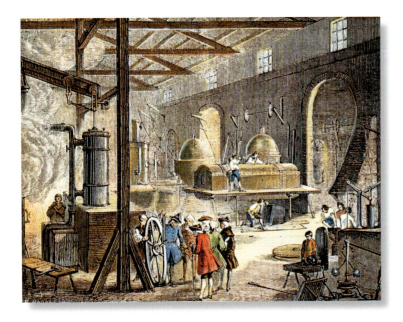

Boulton, Watt & Company made steam engines in this shop in England.

Robert R. Livingston

ROBERT LIVINGSTON WAS BORN IN 1746 into a wealthy New York family. He attended King's College, now Columbia University, in New York. He became a lawyer and was involved in colonial American politics. He took part in the Continental Congress in Philadelphia and helped draft the Declaration of Independence. In 1781, he became the first U.S. secretary of foreign affairs.

In 1801, President Thomas Jefferson sent Livingston to France to represent the United States. It was during his time in France that Livingston met Robert Fulton. Livingston had been interested for years in building a steamboat that could carry people up and down the Hudson River. He knew that if the right boat could be built, it would make a lot of money for its owners. In 1797, he became partners with John Stevens— his sister's husband— and a mechanic named Nicholas Roosevelt. Livingston was a skillful politician. He was able to convince the New York State legislature to give him a **monopoly**. He would be the only person allowed to run steamboats on New York's waterways. The monopoly was given to him on March 27, 1798. It would last for twenty years. Though nothing ever came of this early steamboat partnership, this monopoly would be important in his later partnership with Fulton.

Livingston is also famous for another great success. While representing the United States in France, he helped to make a deal with France. On May 2, 1803, the United States paid France $15 million for the Louisiana Territory. This was a large piece of land west of the Mississippi River. This territory would eventually become all or part of 13 new states. What became known as the Louisiana Purchase doubled the size of the United States.

Chapter Four

The North River Steamboat of Clermont

Interesting Fact

▸ One person who saw the *North River Steamboat's* first trip remembered that some people imagined the boat to be a sea monster. They had never seen anything like it before.

FULTON RETURNED TO THE UNITED STATES and began working on his steamboat project again. He also decided to try to convince the U.S. government to use his underwater weapons. In January 1807, Fulton met with U.S. government officials, who agreed to pay him to show them how to use his weapons. On July 20, he finally succeeded in blowing up a ship after three tries. It took him more than six hours. The U.S. government decided it was not interested, and Fulton finally gave his full attention to the steamboat.

On August 17, 1807, Fulton's steamboat was ready for its first trip. Fulton and his passengers—most of them members of the Livingston family—left New York at 1 P.M. The steamboat was a great success. It traveled the 160 miles from New York City to Albany in 32 hours—an amazing speed of 5 miles per hour! This was an incredible speed in the early 1800s. People along the Hudson River stopped to watch the incredible sight of a steam-powered boat chugging up the river.

When Fulton arrived in Albany, he put a sign on the side of the boat. It advertised that the boat would leave for New York the next day at 9 A.M. Anyone wishing to make the trip could do so for $7. The next morning, five men became Fulton's first paying customers. After that first trip, Fulton knew that his steamboat would make money. He got to work making the steamboat more comfortable for passengers. On September 2, the steamboat began making regular trips between New York City and Albany. On September 3, the steamboat officially

The North River Steamboat *of Clermont traveled regularly between New York City and Albany, New York.*

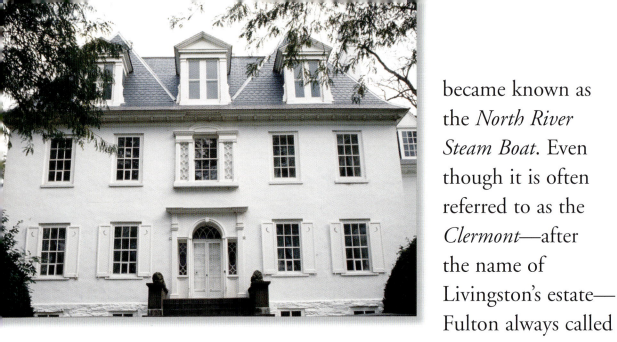

Clermont, built in 1778, was Livingston's home.

Interesting Fact

▸ Harriet Livingston's parents were from well-known, wealthy families. Her mother, Cornelia Schuyler, was a descendant of Peter Schuyler. He was the mayor of Albany in the 1600s. Harriet's father was Walter Livingston. He was Robert Livingston's cousin and owned several thousand acres of land.

became known as the *North River Steam Boat*. Even though it is often referred to as the *Clermont*—after the name of Livingston's estate—Fulton always called it the *North River*.

It is said that Fulton's engagement was announced on that first trip. When the boat had docked at Clermont on August 17, Livingston supposedly told the crowd that Fulton was going to marry Livingston's cousin, Harriet Livingston. They were married in January 1808. They later had three daughters and one son.

The *North River* continued to travel the Hudson over the next few years. Fulton also added other steamboats to make the trip. Eventually, Fulton expanded beyond New York waters. He had always talked of how steamboats would open up the Louisiana Territory. Then, in 1809, he hired Nicholas Roosevelt to study the Ohio and Mississippi

Rivers. In 1810, he told Roosevelt to build a boat in Pittsburgh. When completed, the boat would be taken down to New Orleans, Louisiana. The plan was for it to make regular trips from New Orleans to Natchez, Mississippi. Roosevelt left Pittsburgh on September 27, 1811. The new boat—the *New Orleans*—arrived in New Orleans on January 12, 1812. The boat then began making regular trips between New Orleans and Natchez. Other steamboat projects followed.

The year 1813 was a sad one for Fulton. On February 25, 1813, Robert Livingston suffered a stroke and died. On the same day, Fulton learned that his good friend Joel Barlow had died while in Poland. The steamboat company was also affected by Livingston's death. As Fulton's partner, he

The Port of New Orleans was a very busy place after steamboats became a common way to move goods and people.

The Fulton I *was intended to protect New York City.*

Interesting Fact

▸ The *Fulton I* was never used in battle. The steam warship was moved to the Brooklyn naval yard after the War of 1812. In 1829, an accidental explosion destroyed the ship.

had been the one to take care of all the business. Now other men saw chances to ruin Livingston's monopoly and start their own steamboat routes on the same waters. Fulton had to spend much time and money fighting off these challenges in court.

Fulton briefly returned to his weapons projects when the War of 1812 (1812–1814) broke out, but he had no success. In December 1813, he came up with a project that combined his knowledge of steamboats and his love of weapons: He would build a steam warship. It would float in New York harbor and be ready to defend the city against the British navy. In March 1814, Fulton was given a patent for his warship. He asked the U.S. Congress for money to build the ship. Congress agreed and promised Fulton $1.5 million to build at least one steam warship. The first one would protect the city of New

York. This boat would be named *Fulton I*. Unfortunately, Fulton would not live to see it completed.

In January 1815, Fulton traveled to Trenton, New Jersey, to defend his steamboat patent and his monopoly. The hearing did not go well. His competitors argued that Fulton was not really the true inventor of the steamboat. An angry Fulton stopped in Jersey City on his way home. He wanted to check on the progress of his steam warship, which was being built there. While walking on the frozen river, one of Fulton's friends fell through the ice. Fulton got soaked helping to pull him from the icy water. By the time he got home, he was exhausted and hoarse. He went to bed to rest. After several days, he said he felt better and went to check on the warship again. When he returned to New York, he was very sick. His cough and fever got much worse. The doctors did all they

Interesting Fact

▶ Robert Fulton is buried in the Trinity Church Cemetery in New York City. His body was placed in a Livingston family vault.

The Fulton Monument at Trinity Church in New York City.

Interesting Fact

▸ A postage stamp was issued in 1965 to honor Robert Fulton's 200th birthday.

A bust of Robert Fulton created by French sculptor Jean-Antoine Houdon

could to help him, but nothing worked. Robert Fulton died on February 23, 1815. He was 49 years old.

Many people attended Fulton's funeral at Trinity Church in New York City. Mourners walked along behind the horse-drawn carriage carrying his casket to the church. Guns were fired from the fort at the Battery and from ships in New York harbor to honor Fulton. All mourned the loss of the man whose talent and refusal to give up changed transportation forever. The steamboat opened up the western United States to settlement and development. It was one of the first steps toward the quick and easy movement of people and goods that we take for granted today.

Time LINE

1765 1807 1815

1765 Robert Fulton is born in Pennsylvania on November 14.

1772 The Fulton family farm is sold at auction, and the family returns to Lancaster, Pennsylvania.

1786 Fulton gets sick with a bad cough and goes to a spa to recover.

1787 Fulton leaves the United States and sails to England to learn more about painting.

1794 Fulton is granted his first patent on June 3. It is for his version of the inclined plane.

1796 The paper, *A Treatise on the Improvement of Canal Navigation*, is published.

1797 Fulton moves to Paris and sends his first submarine idea to the French.

1799 Fulton's panorama is built. It becomes his first moneymaking business.

1800 The *Nautilus* appears for the first time on the Seine River in Paris in June.

1801 The French government finally agrees to give Fulton the money he needs to get the *Nautilus* ready for battle.

1802 Fulton meets Robert Livingston, and the two men agree to a steamboat partnership.

1803 Fulton makes his first successful run of a steamboat in August.

1804 Fulton travels to England where he agrees to secretly build underwater weapons to be used against the French.

1806 Fulton returns to the United States to continue work on his steamboat.

1807 The *North River Steam Boat* makes its first trip from New York to Albany on August 17.

1808 Fulton marries Harriet Livingston in January.

1810 Fulton hires Nicholas Roosevelt to build a steamboat that will travel on the Mississippi River.

1814 Fulton is granted a patent and begins building a steam warship.

1815 Robert Fulton dies on February 23 at the age of 49.

Glossary Terms

ambassador (am-BASS-uh-dur)
An ambassador is the top person sent by a government to represent it in another country. Joel Barlow was a U.S. ambassador to Algeria.

apprentice (uh-PREN-tiss)
An apprentice is someone who learns a trade by working with someone who is highly skilled. Robert Fulton learned the skills of miniature painting and hair working by working as a jeweler's apprentice.

auction (AWK-shun)
An auction is a sale at which something is sold to the person who will pay the most for it. When the Fultons could not continue to pay for their farm, they sold it at an auction.

diplomat (DIP-luh-mat)
A diplomat is a person who represents his or her country's government in a foreign country. Robert Livingston was an American diplomat living in France.

inclined planes (in-KLINED PLANES)
Inclined planes are simple machines. It is easier to move heavy objects up the sloped surface of an inclined plane than to try to lift them straight up.

locks (LOKS)
Locks are built in canals in places where boats have to be raised or lowered to meet a different water level. They are confined areas with gates at each end.

monopoly (muh-NOP-eh-lee)
A monopoly means being the only person or company that can sell a product or service. Fulton and Livingston had a monopoly on steamboat travel in the state of New York.

patent (PAT-uhnt)
A patent is a legal document. It gives the inventor of an item the right to be the only person to make or sell the item.

For Further Information

Web Sites

Visit our homepage for lots of links about Robert Fulton:
http://www.childsworld.com/links.html

Note to Parents, Teachers, and Librarians:
We routinely verify our Web links to make sure they're safe, active sites—so encourage your readers to check them out!

Books

Bowen, Andy Russell, and Lisa Harvey (illustrator). *A Head Full of Notions: A Story About Robert Fulton.* Minneapolis: Carolrhoda Books, 1996.

Kroll, Steven, and Bill Farnsworth (illustrator). *Robert Fulton: From Submarine to Steamboat.* New York: Holiday House, 1999.

Pierce, Morris A. *Robert Fulton and the Development of the Steamboat.* New York: PowerKids Press, 2003.

Places to Visit or Contact

Southern Lancaster County Historical Society
To write for more information about the birthplace of Robert Fulton
Box 33
Quarryville, PA 17566

Hudson River Maritime Museum
To learn more about the history of steamboats in New York
One Rondout Landing
Kingston, NY 12401
845/338-0071

Index

American Revolution, 9, 16
Andrews, Jeremiah, 8

Barlow, Joel, 12, 18, 25
Barlow, Ruth, 12, 18
Bonaparte, Napoleón, 12–13, 14, 15
Boulton, Watt & Company, 14, 20
Bourne, William, 16
Bushnell, David, 16

canals, 10–11, 11–12
Clermont (steamboat), 24
Conestoga wagons, 8

Drebel, Cornelius van, 16

Fitch, John, 19
Forfait, Pierre, 14
Fulton, Abraham (brother), 7, 8
Fulton, Elizabeth (sister), 7
Fulton I (steam warship), 26, 27
Fulton, Isabella (sister), 7
Fulton, Mary (sister), 7
Fulton, Mary Smith (mother), 7, 8
Fulton, Robert, Jr.
   art career of, 8, 10
   birth of, 7
   childhood of, 7
   death of, 28
   education of, 7, 8, 9
   health of, 8, 27–28
   marriage of, 24
Fulton, Robert, Sr. (father), 7

George III, king of England, 9

hair working, 8
Hudson River, 19, 21, 23, 24

inclined planes, 11

Jefferson, Thomas, 21

Lancaster, Pennsylvania, 7, 8
Livingston, Harriet, 24
Livingston, Robert, 14, 18, 19, 21, 24, 25

Livingston, Walter, 24
locks, 11
Louisiana Purchase, 21
Louisiana Territory, 21, 24

Mississippi River, 24–25
monopoly, 21, 26, 27

Nautilus (submarine), 14, 15, 20
New Orleans (steamboat) 25
North River Steam Boat, 14, 24
nuclear submarines, 17

Ohio River, 24–25

panorama, 13
Peak Forest Company, 11–12

Roosevelt, Nicholas, 21, 24–25
Royal Academy of Arts, 9

Schuyler, Cornelia, 24
Schuyler, Peter, 24
Stanhope, earl of, 11
steam warships, 26–27
steamboats, 18–19, 20, 21, 22–25, 28
Stevens, John, 21
submarines, 12–13, 13–15, 16–17, 19–20, 22, 26

Thayer, James, 13
torpedoes, 19–20, 22, 26
Treatise on the Improvement of Canal Navigation, A (Robert Fulton), 12
Trinity Church, 27, 28
Turtle (submarine), 16–17

underwater weapons. *See* submarines; torpedoes.
USS *Nautilus* (nuclear submarine), 17

Vanstaphast (investor), 14

War of 1812, 26
Watt, James, 14
West, Benjamin, 8, 9, 10
World War I, 17
World War II, 17